THIS IS ME!

WORDS OF POWER

Edited By Iain McQueen

First published in Great Britain in 2022 by:

YoungWriters® Est. 1991

Young Writers
Remus House
Coltsfoot Drive
Peterborough
PE2 9BF
Telephone: 01733 890066
Website: www.youngwriters.co.uk

All Rights Reserved
Book Design by Ashley Janson
© Copyright Contributors 2021
Softback ISBN 978-1-80015-778-1

Printed and bound in the UK by BookPrintingUK
Website: www.bookprintinguk.com
YB0493L

FOREWORD

For Young Writers' latest competition This Is Me, we asked primary school pupils to look inside themselves, to think about what makes them unique, and then write a poem about it! They rose to the challenge magnificently and the result is this fantastic collection of poems in a variety of poetic styles.

Here at Young Writers our aim is to encourage creativity in children and to inspire a love of the written word, so it's great to get such an amazing response, with some absolutely fantastic poems. It's important for children to focus on and celebrate themselves and this competition allowed them to write freely and honestly, celebrating what makes them great, expressing their hopes and fears, or simply writing about their favourite things. This Is Me gave them the power of words. The result is a collection of inspirational and moving poems that also showcase their creativity and writing ability.

I'd like to congratulate all the young poets in this anthology, I hope this inspires them to continue with their creative writing.

CONTENTS

Brompton-On-Swale CE Primary School, Brompton-On-Swale

Rohan Morrice (9)	1
Skye Cox (10)	2
Freya Wood (10)	4
Olivia Robinson (10)	6
Elizabeth Martin (10)	7
Ava Hustwick (9)	8
Harry Taylor (9)	9
Eve Parr (10)	10
Leah Owen (10)	11
Jorja Knights (10)	12
Jayden Horner (11)	13
Molly Patterson (10)	14
Freddie Simpson (9)	15
William Montgomerie (9)	16
Lewis Weighell (10)	17
Liam Reece Lambert (9)	18
Charlie Miller (9)	19
Dylon Shorleson-Storey	20
Freya Atkinson (9)	21
Sam Carter (9)	22
Annie Brown (9)	23
Faye Olivia Bramley Foster (9)	24
Jake Ethan Bramley Foster (10)	25

Langley Primary School, Solihull

Mayank Karunakar (10)	26
Jacob Giles (7)	28
Zara Phillips (7)	30
Saikrishna Murugappan (7)	31
Jack Jones (7)	32
Grace Capewell (7)	33
Oliver Bradley (7)	34

Lola Plant (7)	35

Newsham Primary School, Blyth

Molly Storey (10)	36
Matthew Toole (10)	37
George Baker (10)	38
Alice Welsh (10)	39
Lilly Carr (10)	40
Zac McSherry (10)	41
Evie Rennison (10)	42
Kate Thomas (11)	43
Maisie English (10)	44
Elizabeth Hood (10)	45
Lily D (10)	46
Jake Harrison (11)	47
Ethan Barnes (10)	48
Jacob Bolam-Brown (10)	49
Ellie Spowart (10)	50
Adam Dixon (10)	51
Emily Wilkes (10)	52
Kenji Tydemen (10)	53
Libby Wood (10)	54
Mason Hicks (10)	55

South Downs Community Special School, Eastbourne

Gracie-Jane Murphy (9)	56
Bradley Dicker (10)	57
IvyLou Devall (8)	58
CJ Tarukwasha (9)	59
Eve Logan-Garrard (9)	60
Daisy Parton (11)	61

Trawden Forest Primary School, Trawden

William Khan (9)	62
Mia Whittam (10)	64
Meghann Uttley (9)	65
Jenna Homby (9)	66
Tilly Feeney (9)	67
Isaac Liam Stockdale (9)	68
Lucas Kitchen (9)	69
Amelia Ross (9)	70
Alfie Smith (9)	71
Mason Baxter (10)	72
Emily Whitaker (9)	73
Max Thompson (9)	74
Theo Gomes (9)	75
Grace Uttley (9)	76
Ibrahim Khan (9)	77
Molly Pickles (9)	78
Noah Nutter (10)	79
Louie Greenwood (9)	80
Patrick Bennett (9)	81

Wybers Wood Academy, Grimsby

Tia Moseley (11)	82
Jackson Waller (10)	83
Leo Crome (9)	84
Charlotte Downes (10)	85
Finley Hodgson (9)	86
Lotti Jane Whitney-Smith (10)	87
Nancy Beatrice (7)	88
Sophie Thompson (10)	90
Isobella Watts (10)	91
Violet Stretton (8)	92
Lucas Turner (9)	93
Chloe Waite (10)	94
Jamie (9)	95
Harry Fletcher (10)	96
Matilda Reveler (10)	97
Bluebell Blow (10)	98
Alana Bouch	99
Isla Stainton (8)	100
Kyan (9)	101
Lilly Davies (9)	102
Harley Rendall-Williams	103
Ella Smith (10)	104
Grace Li	105
Brandon Bore (10)	106
Adam Porter (10)	107
Lila-Blue Smithson (9)	108
Leya Whitley (10)	109
Charlotte Waddingham-Koskie (8)	110
Layla Rendall (11)	111
Isabelle McKerracher (11)	112
Henry Major (11)	113
Arthur H (10)	114
Freddie Fawcett	115
Gracie Callanan (9)	116
Oliver Dee (10)	117
Luke Taylor (11)	118
Jeremiah Blackmore (9)	119
Leyton Jackson (10)	120
Ella Cooper (10)	121
Poppy Oxton (7)	122
Blake Pritchard (9)	123
Rhys Lancaster (10)	124
Kaila Dodd (10)	125
Jack Avison (11)	126
Alfie Sowerby (9)	127
Flynn Westfield (10)	128
Kobi Sellar	129
Lucy Hutchinson (8)	130
Lucas Ardito (10)	131
Elsie Jackson (11)	132
Riley D (10)	133
Ronny Roberts (10)	134
Izabelle Norman (10)	135
Emily Mai (8)	136
Lilly Waller (7)	137
Olly Holgate (8)	138
Erika Ioana (7)	139
Izabelle Blanchard (7)	140
Amber Whitney-Smith (9)	141
Lily Dodds (8)	142
Harry Smith (10)	143

Name	No.
Daisy Dodds (10)	144
Honey-May Bradley (10)	145
Charlotte Porter (8)	146
Elizabeth Atter (9)	147
Olivia Swales (7)	148
Heston Bloomfield (10)	149
Maisie Sowerby (10)	150
Jack Hillman (11)	151
Sophia Waddingham-Koskie (11)	152
Freddie Croudson (10)	153
Erin Dalton (7)	154
Aaliyah Porritt (10)	155
Charlie Brindley (10)	156
Marley Hallam (10)	157
Florence Gallagher (7)	158
Harrison Drinkell (9)	159
Sophie Brown (10)	160
Nahla Ingram (7)	161
Freya Dee (7)	162
Seren Saunders (8)	163
Leona Cutting (9)	164
Dolly Barker Johnstone (8)	165
Maicey Bateman (10)	166
Ellie Clough (8)	167
Olivia Westerman (8)	168
Levi Whitton (8)	169
Riley Waters (9)	170
Dexter Todd	171
Oscar Thompson (7)	172
Thomas Mills (10)	173
Harley Oakshatt (7)	174
Jacob Taylor (8)	175
Oscar Capindale (7)	176
Isla Penny Anderson-Bright (7)	177
Elianna Greetham (7)	178
George Mazingham (7)	179
Daisy Grimble-Wright (7)	180
Kealan Croft (8)	181
Archie (9)	182
William Lewis (7)	183
Ava Kirwan (8)	184
Walter Holdsworth (8)	185
Chloe Smith (7)	186
Freddie Colyer (7)	187
Millie McKerracher (8)	188
Darren Richardson (8)	189
Hattie Acquorff (8)	190
Mason Howarth (9)	191
Lucas Freeman (10)	192
Oliver Smith (8)	193
Kyle White (9)	194
Milla Robinson (7)	195
Hannah Tobis (8)	196
Jack Ward (8)	197
Theo Porter (8)	198
Harry Corke (8)	199
Grace Hydes (8)	200
Benji West (8)	201
Hayden Wood (8)	202
Ben Lawson (7)	203
Lyla Reid (9)	204
Albert Holdsworth (8)	205
Olivia Harris (8)	206
Charlie Crome (8)	207
Isaac George Woolsey (7)	208
Phoebe Spendlow (7)	209
Rose Dodds (7)	210
Amelia Peacock (8)	211
Reuben MacFarlane (8)	212
Evie Parker (8)	213
Beau Shore (9)	214
Honey-Rae Phillips (8)	215
Thomas Ayres (8)	216
Olly Ranyard (8)	217
Esmai Rendall (7)	218
Jacob Burton (8)	219
Jayden Lister (8)	220
Isabella Grainger (7)	221
Frankie Leahy (8)	222

THE POEMS

My Pug Poem

Pugs' eyes are as bright as the sun and they are very cuddly and fun,
As fast as a Lamborghini but as light as a feather,
Paws as strong as leather, eyes as bright as emerald and claws as sharp as knives,
Nice and cuddly and very jumpy,
And a face that's very bumpy,
Eyes as emerald and terrible teeth,
Very yappy and very happy but don't be unkind or they will be a bit snappy and very unhappy,
Pugs are not smelly but their bellies jiggle like jelly,
I will let you in on a secret, pugs love telly,
Pugs are not lazy but they are crazy,
Pugs are not aliens because they don't shoot lasers,
And pugs are not police because they don't shoot tasers,
Pugs have curly tails but they're as slow as snails,
And like humans they have males,
And pugs do not look like seals,
And they are as strong as steel.

Rohan Morrice (9)
Brompton-On-Swale CE Primary School, Brompton-On-Swale

This Is Me

Roses are red,
Violets are blue,
Hello there, nice to meet you,
I'm Skye, my age is ten,
I hope to become your new best friend,

My star sign is Sagittarius, my Chinese is the tiger,
Don't mess with me, my element is fire,
Jupiter is my zodiac's planet, big bold and strong,
My sign's god is Zeus, so nothing could go wrong,

I'm obsessed with Marvel, all the big booms
My favourite is Loki, you could say I'm mischievous too,
I've watched him use his staff like it's a toy,
He's the best, Marvel boy,

My favourite colour is gorgeous green,
It shimmers like a shamrock, but gold, so bright and beautiful,
My book of life is full of adventure, so many trees,
Green peas, life is a treasure,

I have hazel-brown hair, awesome and wavy,
My eyes are orange tiger stripes baby,
I have pure skin, thick like a turtle shell,
I have a book-filled room as well,

I'm a huge kitten fan, I have a huge cat fam,
We love to hug our kittens, they are cute and adorable,
But lazy, what a pity.

Skye Cox (10)
Brompton-On-Swale CE Primary School, Brompton-On-Swale

This Is Me

I am a lightning bolt in football boots
I have a Marvel and football filled room
My Zodiac sign is an Aquarius
My best friend is a Sagittarius
My element is air
So I love to fly because I just don't care

My Chinese sign is a bunny
So that is why I am sporty and funny
Aquarius is the leader of Uranus and Jupiter
So that is why I am funnier
I am a huge Marvel fan
I would love a Marvel van

Marvel is the best
So I can defeat all Marvel tests
I am as brave as a tiger
I want to be a hero like Captain America
I love to play football
I am so quick so I can get past you all

I am a rapid right wing
I like to read things
My favourite book is 'Grandpa's Great Escape'
I love to cook and bake
My sister and I love an adventure
That is why we always find treasure.

Freya Wood (10)
Brompton-On-Swale CE Primary School, Brompton-On-Swale

My Favourite Animal Riddle

It hurdles up hay so be careful from afar
He's a lighting bolt so be cautious where you are
He's a car, tall and wide so quickly hides
When he swims he kicks from behind
It has four legs and loves grass
He wears a super saddle most days
He is a graceful grey and shines in the sunset every day
He's an amazing animal
Imagine him jumping really high
About ninety centimetres is his maximum height
He can jump as far as the world
He loves to gallop across fields for fun
He loves to cuddle all day
The night is his favourite time of day
What am I?

Answer: A horse.

Olivia Robinson (10)
Brompton-On-Swale CE Primary School, Brompton-On-Swale

My Family

My family is as marvellous as a flower,
My dog is as white as snow,
My mum and nana have hearts of gold,
My pets are entertaining,
They are my fabulous sunshine,
Our family is a patchwork quilt,
My little white wolf and chunky Charlie are the best,
My excellent Edward, magnificent mummy and nice nana are amazing,
My mum's eyes are delightful diamonds,
My nana's smile is amazing,
My brother's laugh is hilarious,
My brother loves Minecraft, Pokémon and Mario,
My mum loves bees and family,
My nana loves nature and family.

Elizabeth Martin (10)
Brompton-On-Swale CE Primary School, Brompton-On-Swale

My Life

My life is a rollercoaster of emotions
I love piglets, they're the best
My favourite season is Christmas because I love giving
If you have a pool party I'm straight in
My favourite hobbies are swimming and gaming
I have a big family
My favourite subject is art
If you didn't see a picture of a micropig
They're so cute
I am an animal lover
I love school, my teachers are the best
Piglets are pretty posh
When I run I am as slow as a sloth
Finally, my heart is made of gold.

Ava Hustwick (9)
Brompton-On-Swale CE Primary School, Brompton-On-Swale

Pikachu

Pikachu is as fast as a lightning bolt
He is adorable, warning don't cuddle or it will electrocute you
Pikachu's moves are thunderbolt, electroball, agility, thundershock and volt tackle
Now I would say Pikachu is a good partner
He's the perfect Pokémon
That's my friend Pikachu for you
Pikachu is an electric type
Pichu was first, then Pikachu, then Raichu
Did you know there are legendary and mythical Pokémon?
Like Dialga, Hoopa, Moltres, Blue Latias, Red Latias and Darkrai.

Harry Taylor (9)
Brompton-On-Swale CE Primary School, Brompton-On-Swale

Animals

My delightful dream is to own a hilarious horse
I will train it to go over jiggly jumps
My dog is a sprinter and my horse will be called Winter
My dog may be dainty but he is determined
If he gets excited he will make you nervous
My dog is a fluffy, fun fellow
He has bouncy brown eyes and has a heart of gold
My horse will be the love of my life and she will shine as bright as gold
My will is beaming brown like my dog
Oh did I mention my dog's name is Tip.

Eve Parr (10)
Brompton-On-Swale CE Primary School, Brompton-On-Swale

This Is Me

I like having fun in the sun,
I love cheesy pizza but not from the freezer,
My shopping bags are like tornadoes and at the bottom is a bag of Doritos,
Skating across the ice rink with my headphones which are pink,
My hamster is like the rat from Ratatouille, keeping me up at night chewing,
Harry Potter is the best and way better than all the rest,
My eyes are diamonds shining in the sun,
My dog thinks he's a tiger, tearing up his toys,
Now you know this is me.

Leah Owen (10)
Brompton-On-Swale CE Primary School, Brompton-On-Swale

This Is Me

T he best people in the world are superstar Skye, fantastic Freya and amazing Anna,
H i, I'm joyful Jorja, nice to meet you,
I n my zodiac Cancer mind, I will leave you behind,
S o many emotions come spilling around,

I love Marvel, Thor is the best and he is better than the rest,
S o don't mess about, just stand tall,

M y Chinese is bunny, my element is water,
E veryone tell me what you are.

Jorja Knights (10)
Brompton-On-Swale CE Primary School, Brompton-On-Swale

All About Fishing

F ishing is the best,
I have caught fish as big as a grown man,
S aturdays are the best fishing days,
H appiness is when you have a fish on the rod,
I love fishing,
N o matter what, fishing comes first,
G host carp are one of my favourite fish

R eeling in the fish as I wait to see the surprise,
O ver fifteen fish caught in one day,
D amp rainy days are the best.

Jayden Horner (11)
Brompton-On-Swale CE Primary School, Brompton-On-Swale

This Is Me

You will need
A room of teddies
100g of helpfulness
A drop of kindness
A million grams of silliness
A brother

Now you need to
Put your brother in the bin so he doesn't ruin it
Secondly, get your room of teddies and add 100g of helpfulness
A drop of kindness
And a touch of silliness
Finally, put it in the oven until it is bubbling
Take your brother out of the bin (optional).

Molly Patterson (10)
Brompton-On-Swale CE Primary School, Brompton-On-Swale

My Favourite Animal

A creature of land and can live for long in the water,
It cannot fly or so I think,
But it can jump high into the sky,
It's as green as the grass,
Its legs are as long as a snake and it lays its tiny eggs in the lake,
It lives in the darkest and dampest of places,
It's an accurate amphibian, yet as precious as a pearl,
With eyes like diamonds,
My favourite animal is...
A frog!

Freddie Simpson (9)
Brompton-On-Swale CE Primary School, Brompton-On-Swale

Ying And Yang The Poem

This poem is about two gerbils called Ying and Yang
He is as small as a mouse but cuter
It is Ying
See them dig as fast as lightning
In their cottage, it is as dark as Yang
But as cuddly as both of them
See them cutely cuddled up
My sister looks after the two gerbils
Who are as white as snow and dark as night
Eventually, they go fast to sleep.

William Montgomerie (9)
Brompton-On-Swale CE Primary School, Brompton-On-Swale

What Am I?

I'm cute and fluffy
My eyes are like mini diamonds
I'm as brave as a ferocious lion
I'm as fast as a cheetah
If you scare me I'll run away like a lightning bolt
I am adorable like a pug
I'm as little as a bunny
But as lazy as a hippo
My fur is as fluffy as candyfloss
What am I?

Answer: I'm a kitten.

Lewis Weighell (10)
Brompton-On-Swale CE Primary School, Brompton-On-Swale

Sausage Dog

The dog is as thick as a 5000-year-old tree,
He has hilarious, crazy hair,
He is very fast,
He is very bouncy and he loves the bin,
We call him Tiny Tim,
His fluff is velvety and he is very cute,
He has eyes like diamonds,
He is a pig when it comes to food,
He gobbles it up like a gorilla.

Liam Reece Lambert (9)
Brompton-On-Swale CE Primary School, Brompton-On-Swale

Rugby

Run to the other side
Dive on the line
To score the best try
It is best to tackle below the waist
If he's a bit chubby, get him by the feet and he will collapse
I am as fast as lightning so when I run I am just a black blur
So I score the best tries and I am the best tackler on the pitch.

Charlie Miller (9)
Brompton-On-Swale CE Primary School, Brompton-On-Swale

What Am I?

I am cute
I am lazy
I live in Asia
I am very vicious
My food is very delicious
I am very sleepy
Do you know yet?
I will keep on going
I was founded in 1801
I live in the hills
I have lots of trees where I live
What am I?

Answer: A red panda.

Dylon Shorleson-Storey
Brompton-On-Swale CE Primary School, Brompton-On-Swale

Freya

- **F** erocious, fabulous footballer who is always on the move
- **R** ocky is my delightful dog, he's as greedy as a menacing gorilla
- **E** xquisite, excellent Everton is who I support
- **Y** et I have a precious heart of glorious gold
- **A** s fast as Usain Bolt.

Freya Atkinson (9)
Brompton-On-Swale CE Primary School, Brompton-On-Swale

My Reindeer Poem

I am brown and have jingly bells on my harnesses
I have antlers and have nine friends
We all help Santa deliver the presents
There are lots of elves to help
My name begins with R
What am I?

Answer: A reindeer.

Sam Carter (9)
Brompton-On-Swale CE Primary School, Brompton-On-Swale

What Am I?

I am slow and still
Slimy and slithery with a silky shell
I love to eat and love to slither
I love to glimmer and I love to shimmer
I carry my home on my back.
What am I?

Answer: A snail.

Annie Brown (9)
Brompton-On-Swale CE Primary School, Brompton-On-Swale

Faye

F abulous, bouncy basketball player
A stonishing at delightful horse riding like Charlotte Diyar
Y et I have a heart of glorious gold
E ndearing Ebb is my dashing, daunting dog.

Faye Olivia Bramley Foster (9)
Brompton-On-Swale CE Primary School, Brompton-On-Swale

What Am I?

I am as quiet as a German Shorthaired Pointer
I am as accurate as an eagle
I am as patient as a dog
I am as dangerous as a golden eagle
What am I?

Answer: A hunter.

Jake Ethan Bramley Foster (10)
Brompton-On-Swale CE Primary School, Brompton-On-Swale

This Is Me

When I grow up,
I want to make things up,
Out of wood, metal and brick,

When I work,
I do it with all I've got,
And only then, I do a lot,

I like riding my bike,
And I also take long hikes,

When I become an engineer,
I want to be successful in my career,

One day I might create something swell,
Just like Alexander Graham Bell

Painting is a good activity,
Because it unleashes creativity,

When I am bored,
My mind will soar,
To a daisyland-like scene,
Where nothing is mean,

I like building models,
And drawing too,
But if I draw too much,
My mind will go a bit coo-coo,

When I am sad,
There will always be something to make me glad,
Through and through,
Always in what I do,

Spiders scare me but not too much,
But my mum won't hesitate to get a brush,

I love nature,
The grass, the field, those green pastures,

This is me,
And this, I am proud to be,

I love music,
Especially pop,
I rarely listen to it,
But I also like rock.

Mayank Karunakar (10)
Langley Primary School, Solihull

This Is Me

My name is Jacob and my last name is Giles,
I have blonde hair, brown eyes and a big cheeky smile,
I love to spend time with my friends and family,
Playing games and laughing, helping out gladly,
I enjoy playing football and I'm really good at swimming,
Running and splashing, my face aches from grinning,
I love playing outside with my brother and dad,
Skateboarding and scooting, so much fun to be had,
When I'm unwinding at home and my thumbs start to twitch,
I have adventures and build things on my Nintendo Switch,
There are so many things that I like to do,
Making dens on the sofa and watching YouTube,
Video games give me ideas of what I might want to be,
Flying planes, driving trains or a captain at sea,

Only scratching the surface of what could fit in this poem,
So I'll leave it here or I'll just keep on going,
This is me.

Jacob Giles (7)
Langley Primary School, Solihull

This Is Me

My name is Zara and I am kind, beautiful and clever
When I'm older I want to be a primary school teacher
I believe in myself and when I can't do something I tell myself that I can do it
What is special and individual about me is that I have Afro-Caribbean hair
My superpower is when I take my hair out
It looks like a lion's mane
Which makes me feel strong
I am energetic, excitable and joyful
Mom thinks I'm delightful
My dream is to have a dog one day
So I can take him out to play
I am passionate about helping people with COVID-19
This is something that made me very poorly and I had to go to the hospital for it
So I want to help people who have it.

Zara Phillips (7)
Langley Primary School, Solihull

Delighted

D addy brings me my favourite food
E aster eggs are the best
L ove spending time with my family
I n autumn finding acorns and conkers
G etting together with my friends
H appy holidays, Halloween and all
T asting yummy spicy food
E vening walks along the beach
D esserts are the best.

Saikrishna Murugappan (7)
Langley Primary School, Solihull

Super Jack Number Ten

Sunday morning is my favourite day
Today's the day I get to play
Twice a week I have to train
No matter the weather, sunshine or rain
Knowle Lions is my team
The greatest team the world has seen
Today I hope to score again
Super Jack number ten
It makes my day when we win, I dream to play like John McGinn.

Jack Jones (7)
Langley Primary School, Solihull

Me And My Future

I look to my future and guess what I see?
It's me with my own personality,
My own colour hair,
The way I sometimes overcare,
From my head to my toes,
And what I smell through my nose,
I am as precious as can be,
All of these things make up me,
So let's work together and be happy,
This is me.

Grace Capewell (7)
Langley Primary School, Solihull

This Is Me

My name is Ollie!
I love macaroni!
I'm great when it comes to Lego.
I'd say I'm a master, because I go faster.
Oh, and I really love pasta!

Oliver Bradley (7)
Langley Primary School, Solihull

Pony

Pony
Pretty, cute, soft
Whinnying, jogging, galloping
My sensitive buddy
Chuckles.

Lola Plant (7)
Langley Primary School, Solihull

This Is Me

I am a daughter to Kerri and Mick
I am a niece to Anthony and Stephen
I am a big sister to Ben
I am a little sister to Jamie and Chloe

I love being silly
I love ice cream, especially vanilla, sometimes it gives me shivers
I love singing and acting
I love football and flowers
I love my best friends and my family too

I dislike people getting sad or very mad
I dislike when my brother annoys me
I dislike when people are not kind or give me a fright

I have a dog called Daisy but when she barks it gives me a headache
My favourite food is chicken korma and my name is Molly
My inspiration is a lot of different singers.

Molly Storey (10)
Newsham Primary School, Blyth

This Is Me

I love to read
I love to write
I love to sing all day and night
I love my family
I like my friends
I like to play with my sister and friends
I like to watch Netflix and YouTube
I think of myself as loving and caring
I don't like bananas or football but that's okay because no one is the same
My dream is to become a fashion designer because I love the colour and patterns
I love my primary school teachers and friends
I love to eat pizza especially pepperoni
I love vacations because they're fun and adventurous
This is Matthew.

Matthew Toole (10)
Newsham Primary School, Blyth

This Is Me

Hey you right there
Look at me
I'm the best, can't you see
I like a lot about me
For example
Video games, football and of course
Hate all of the haters
I have a celebrity crush
But we'll talk about that later

I have a sister
I also have a mama
I do go lala
Sometimes
About my dream
To be a football commentator

My favourite time of the week is a Saturday
I get out and play with my friends, yay
My dream is to play in the Premier League
Maybe one day I'll be in the Champions League.

George Baker (10)
Newsham Primary School, Blyth

The Poem About Me

Cute cuddly animals make me happy
My brother is mean to me I hate it
Drawing is calming to me, it makes me happy
I'm a rockstar queen
Going to the front makes me scream
Writing gets my attention, it's good
I don't like maths, it's too confusing
I love crafting, it's so fun
Not being able to do something angers me
Electronics keep me from being bored
Food is my life
Doing work is a bit boring
Hot chocolate is delicious
Lego is fun to play with
This is me.

Alice Welsh (10)
Newsham Primary School, Blyth

This Is Me

I like my family
I like to read
I like my friends
I like doing English as well

I'm a big and little sister
I am also a cousin to fifteen kids
I do dance and dance competitions for thousands of people

I don't like football or cold places
I also don't like vegetables like peas and broccoli
I also live with my mum, dad, siblings too
When I'm older I want to be a doctor, if not a hairdresser
My favourite colours are red and blue.

Lilly Carr (10)
Newsham Primary School, Blyth

This Is Me

This recipe will tell you how to make Zac McSherry

You will need
Comedy
Dog lover
Bisexuality
Paddleboarding
Baker
Adventurer
Lots of hair
Friendliness
Butter and sugar

Instructions
Add 50g of butter
Add three tablespoons of sugar
Whisk for five minutes
Cook at 100 degrees for six to eight minutes
Leave to cool for ten minutes
Add baking and whisk for three minutes
Add 300g of bisexuality whilst whisking.

Zac McSherry (10)
Newsham Primary School, Blyth

This Is Me

One bucket of my best friend Maisie
Two cups of hugs
A glass of love
Five spoons of art
A bucket of my family
A bowl of dance
Six bowls of desserts
A cup of fruit and veg
A cup of baking
One bucket of my best friend Emely
Two bowls of kindness
A bucket of becoming a brain surgeon
A bowl of weird
A bucket of my dog
This is me.

Evie Rennison (10)
Newsham Primary School, Blyth

This Is Me

K icking Kate playing football
A crobatic Kate doing gymnastics
T alking Kate is crazy
E xercising Kate playing basketball

L oving Kate is with her friends
E nergising Kate ready for football
I like football
G oing football crazy
H appy Kate is obsessed with football.

Kate Thomas (11)
Newsham Primary School, Blyth

This Is Me

One scoop of art
One handful of horse riding
One cup full of my weirdo BFF
One spoonful of my dad Fred
One teaspoon of my brilliant mum
One basketful of love
One jug of my pets
One bucket of hopes and dreams
One cup of my family
One basket of being an architect
And this is me.

Maisie English (10)
Newsham Primary School, Blyth

All About Me

A bucket of drama,
A teaspoon of weakness,
A bag full of strength,
A bucket of tiredness,
A shoe full of strength,
A cup of meanness,
A powerful drop of believing,

Get a round bowl,
And put everything in carefully,
Get a spoon,
And finally mix, then done.

Elizabeth Hood (10)
Newsham Primary School, Blyth

This Is Me

T ruthful for people
H appy life
I love my guinea pigs
S o I'm getting my hair cut soon

I ndependent
S loth

M y life is full of friends
E njoying time with friends.

Lily D (10)
Newsham Primary School, Blyth

All About Me

T errible at English
H appy when I get things right
I love dogs
S illy at times

I rritate my sister
S ports are the best

M otorbikes are cool
E xcellent at maths.

Jake Harrison (11)
Newsham Primary School, Blyth

This Is Me
A kennings poem

I am a
Lobster eater
Gaming lover
Bike racer
Good learner
Cake taster
Netflix watcher
Lolly licker
Amazing sleeper
Excellent listener
Responsible worker
YouTube watcher
Excellent defender.

Ethan Barnes (10)
Newsham Primary School, Blyth

This Is Me

A sprinkle of intelligence
A gallon full of kindness
A shovel full of aliveness
A sea of football
A bag full of rugby
A pool full of creativity
A river full of attitude
A hot tub of food
A cup full of weird.

Jacob Bolam-Brown (10)
Newsham Primary School, Blyth

Recipe For Me

A gallon of family
A cup of dance
A bucket of kindness
A waterfall of love
A lake of smiles
A cup of smartness
A bucket of sparkles
A cup of sunshine
And last but not least, a best friend.

Ellie Spowart (10)
Newsham Primary School, Blyth

This Is Me

Add a cup of fun
Add a cup of football
Add a teaspoon of gaming
Add a bit of school
Add some outside
Add a slice of pepperoni pizza
Add a cup full of books
A load of smiles
This is me.

Adam Dixon (10)
Newsham Primary School, Blyth

This Is Me

A kennings poem

I am a
Football watcher
Chocolate eater
Deep sleeper
Hard worker
Fruit lover
Make-up hater
Wild walker
Dog lover
Food lover
And the best thing about me is
Being me.

Emily Wilkes (10)
Newsham Primary School, Blyth

This Is Me

I am the bigger brother to Tommy
I am the son of Alan and Ally
I am the nephew to Petrica and Sonia
I am the cousin to Kierin, Cameron and Chloe
I am the grandson of Susan and Dennis
This is me.

Kenji Tydemen (10)
Newsham Primary School, Blyth

This Is Me
A kennings poem

I am a
Book reader
Spider catcher
Big dreamer
Savoury eater
TV watcher
Clumsy walker
Happy smiler
Animal lover
Deep sleeper
And my best talent is
Being me.

Libby Wood (10)
Newsham Primary School, Blyth

This Is Me

A kennings poem

Piggy player
Monkey watcher
Cool coder
Slime reacher
Mario maker
Roblox gamer
Binge snack enjoyer
This is me.

Mason Hicks (10)
Newsham Primary School, Blyth

Gracie

G racie loves,
R acing bikes in the field,
A nimals and unicorns and my,
C at's name is Prince,
I ce cream, I love the strawberry flavour,
E ve is my best friend.

Gracie-Jane Murphy (9)
South Downs Community Special School, Eastbourne

What Bradley Likes

I like computer games, but not dogs
I like visiting friends, but not cats
I like reading, but not snakes
I like art, but not foxes
I like a lot of things
But not all things.

Bradley Dicker (10)
South Downs Community Special School, Eastbourne

What I Like

I like fish and chips, but not roast dinner
I like white, but not pasta
I like pizza, but not dancing
I like swimming but not art
I like a lot of things
But not all things.

IvyLou Devall (8)
South Downs Community Special School, Eastbourne

CJ

C ake
J uice

C ake
U gly fruit
T omato
H amburger
B anana
E gg
R adish
T oast.

CJ Tarukwasha (9)
South Downs Community Special School, Eastbourne

What Eve Likes

I like pizza, but not eggs
I like pink but not black
I like football but not dancing
I like art but not writing
I like a lot of things
But not all things.

Eve Logan-Garrard (9)
South Downs Community Special School, Eastbourne

Daisy

D inner is yum
A rt is good
I love pink
S wimming is fun
Y ellow I love.

Daisy Parton (11)
South Downs Community Special School, Eastbourne

It's Monday Again

I wake up early in the morning instead of snoring
I realise it's the weekend, my life is great, full of fate
I reach for my door
I start to snore
I start to fall asleep
In a beep
I open my eyes
It turns out it wasn't pleasing
I was dreaming
I look at my clock in shock
I remember it's Monday
I go downstairs, start to stare
Where's my breakfast?
Never mind breakfast
You're gonna be late
I push upstairs
Looking for my school uniform
I couldn't find it
The day has come to an end
It was a big bend

I get grounded and sent to my room
All I find is a broom
To clean up my mess
I feel like I'm under arrest
I'm as kind as a sloth
But silly like a moth.

William Khan (9)
Trawden Forest Primary School, Trawden

My Life

Me with hair as dark as chocolate
Watching little butterflies in my garden
After gaming and playing, adopt me with my friends
Time for my favourite time, putting on PJs
Dreaming about the Titanic movie, it's my favourite
My eyes the colour of grass awaiting
In the shower singing all the greatest hits
Time for school to make my dream of becoming an actress come true if I work hard
Daisie telling me I'm kind and passionate
Keira and I talking about Jack and Rose again
Emily when it's lunchtime
This is my life.

Mia Whittam (10)
Trawden Forest Primary School, Trawden

All About Me

I am a superstar dancer,
I am as rapid as a cheetah,
I am a dog lover,
I have light brown hair like a monkey,
I dress like a fashion stylist,
I am as smart as a tuxedo penguin,
I love nothing much but playing with my guinea pig,
I am smaller than my annoying twin sister but taller than a toddler,
My iPhone is nothing but electrical wires,
My dad has a car with tyres,
I love a good laugh,
And having a good bath.

Meghann Uttley (9)
Trawden Forest Primary School, Trawden

Holiday Time

H oliday time, it is going to be so cool
O cean blue, can't wait to dive in
L oving the sizzling sand between my toes
I n the hole I dug up five minutes ago
D aylight is so pretty here
A wesome isn't it
Y es I found a seashell, a pretty one too

T ime to go
I love it here though
M y mum gives me ice cream
E veryone likes ice cream.

Jenna Homby (9)
Trawden Forest Primary School, Trawden

My Swimming

S wimming is the best
W ith all my friends
I t is all wet and fun
M y swimming teacher is the best because she helps me learn
M y mum is the best for coming with me to swimming
I like swimming because I can jump and dive in
N o, I don't like getting water up my nose but I still like swimming
G ood job I know how to swim otherwise I wouldn't have all this fun.

Tilly Feeney (9)
Trawden Forest Primary School, Trawden

All About Me

A good BMX stunter
L ittle like a puppy
L oving like a cat

A nd a very good drawer
B ecause of my mum and dad, I have a home
O ffering sweets, I'll take three
U nless it's sunny I'm at the beach
T ins of beans are my favourite food

M e and William stick together like pizza and chips
E veryone is unique just like me.

Isaac Liam Stockdale (9)
Trawden Forest Primary School, Trawden

World's Greatest Striker

I'm a star on a football pitch,
As fast as sound,
No one will tackle me on the ground,
I'm a superhuman striker,
I'm the best,
I never rest,
CR7 is gone,
From the world, I lay upon,
I take the Captain's armband,
Ready to pounce,
Out onto the football pitch,
I bounce,
Champions league is the best,
Lifting the trophy is my destiny.

Lucas Kitchen (9)
Trawden Forest Primary School, Trawden

Horse Carer

- **H** appiness time with Bravo
- **O** pen stable
- **R** espectfully brush him
- **S** it down with hot chocolate, it's cold outside
- **E** agerly watch him get apples out of his hay net
- **C** arrot time, yum
- **A** nnoyingly offer my horse ten minutes of field time
- **R** ide time
- **E** vie my sister comes to brush her horse
- **R** est time!

Amelia Ross (9)
Trawden Forest Primary School, Trawden

This Is Me

A lfie is my name
D ad is a family member
V ery excited about bike-ability
E llie is my sister's name
N oah is a name
T heo is my friend's name
U nder the sea, sharks are swimming
R ome is a place
O h no
U ranus is a planet
S ensibility is an emotion.

Alfie Smith (9)
Trawden Forest Primary School, Trawden

My Year

As friendly as a bird
Smart as an elephant
Chilled like a polar bear
I feel dry like the desert
My eye burns in the light
My sight is bright
My life is in your sight
My friends are like a book
I have many different looks
I'm stuck
In a truck
That's a duck
My life is never stuck
I'm going up.

Mason Baxter (10)
Trawden Forest Primary School, Trawden

Me

A chicken dinner is my favourite food
W riting is my second favourite lesson
E mily is my name
S pace is my favourite thing
O utside is the best place to be
M aking cakes with my grandma is always fun
E lephants are my favourite animal.

Emily Whitaker (9)
Trawden Forest Primary School, Trawden

I Love Football

F ati plays for Barcelona
O ffside by a tiny bit
O ut of play by a centimetre
T onight is Messi's debut
B ang it's a screamer
A through ball
L ukaku scored top bins
L uke Shaw on the volley.

Max Thompson (9)
Trawden Forest Primary School, Trawden

The Weekend Is Coming

Friday is ascending by the minute
And the weekend slowly comes
As the clocks tick, half-past three is on the move
It feels like precious hours have been by
Then the bell rings, I'm as happy as can be
As I head home I say bye Friday, hello weekend!

Theo Gomes (9)
Trawden Forest Primary School, Trawden

Me

My eyes are as green as grass
My hair is as blonde as sand
My legs are as long as giants'
My lips are as red as roses
My eyebrows are as brown as chocolate
My ears are as smooth as a fluffy blanket
What am I?

Answer: Me.

Grace Uttley (9)
Trawden Forest Primary School, Trawden

This Is Me

I 'm very good at doing bike tricks
B alancing on one wheel
R unning like the wind
A way from the chaser
H appy with friends
I nterested in animals
M aking cakes with my mum.

Ibrahim Khan (9)
Trawden Forest Primary School, Trawden

Me

A lover of animals,
A superstar baker,
As crazy as a dog,
As fearless as a lion,
My hair is chocolate-brown,
I love to dance so sing along,
I have a passion for fashion,
This is me!

Molly Pickles (9)
Trawden Forest Primary School, Trawden

When I'm On My Bike

When I'm on my bike, I have lots of fun
Riding up and down the track
I do big jumps and little ones too
And whilst I'm doing it I shout wahoo
So people can hear me from a mile or two.

Noah Nutter (10)
Trawden Forest Primary School, Trawden

Gaming

G ood at video games
A cracked out gamer
M y favourite game mode on Fortnite is the pit
I like Fortnite the best
N o noobs
G ood gamer.

Louie Greenwood (9)
Trawden Forest Primary School, Trawden

The Best Ingredients Of Me

How to make me
Sprinkle a bit of joy
Maybe a joke or two
And some mystery
Add some sugar too
With Internet memes
Enjoy the show because you made me!

Patrick Bennett (9)
Trawden Forest Primary School, Trawden

All About Me

T o begin with, my friends describe me as,
I ntelligent, kind,
A nd honest like my BFFs are to me,

M y favourite colours, purple and yellow, or anything glittery,
O n my trampoline is one of the times when I'm most happy,
S ome day I want to become a fashion designer,
E nglish and maths are my favourite subjects,
L earning new things is my speciality,
E njoying being unique,
Y ou should now know all about me.

Tia Moseley (11)
Wybers Wood Academy, Grimsby

This Is Me

Do you really think I wanna rap these lyrics in rhyme
For you to see the good side of me
All I ever will care about is family
And I will know when my sister looks at me with glee

I'm not gonna rap one syllable
But y'all should, would, could
I would and probably should
Say what they call me
J-dog
They say I am a cheetah in disguise
RIP them people who think it's lies
They say I'm a beast in the algorithm
The combination is the cheat code.

Jackson Waller (10)
Wybers Wood Academy, Grimsby

Halloween

H alloween, a time of ghouls, ghosts and witches
A time the entire world is released from the grave
L ong last pumpkins are howling with joy
L ast of the spirits released from the underworld
O ne night only can we be awoken from our torture
W eeks, months, years, we lay in the dirt, now we rise for revenge
E veryone knows we're gone but not for long
E veryone fears us, no one is safe
N ow it is time for Halloween!

Leo Crome (9)
Wybers Wood Academy, Grimsby

This Is Me

Hi my name is Charlotte
And I am ten
I live in Grimsby
But not in a den

Life in my house is really crazy
My brother won't stop annoying me
My mum and dad work and work
And I just sit on my phone every day

My likes and my dislikes are kind of weird
I like the subjects PE and writing
And here are two of my dislikes, onions and burgers
I also like friends and pets, my fears are heights and spiders
And that is me, I hope you enjoyed it.

Charlotte Downes (10)
Wybers Wood Academy, Grimsby

This Is Me

F ootball is the best,
I 'm good at maths,
N o one can get past me in football,
L ove science and writing,
E agles are the best,
Y ellow and blonde hair.

H ave skills in football,
O vals are unusual,
D oing hard work makes success,
G oing to school is good,
S ome things are tricky,
O ther things are simple,
N o one is better than me at maths.

Finley Hodgson (9)
Wybers Wood Academy, Grimsby

This Is Me

T illy, Pixie, Gracie are the names of my cats,
H orses are my favourite animal, that's one of my facts,
I love my five-man fam, my brother, my sister, my mum and my dad,
S ad is what I rarely am.

I am crazy, cool, kind, helpful, honest and fun,
S illy club is where I belong.

M arshmallow and Popcorn are the names of my gerbils,
E ager is what I am when it comes to animals.

Lotti Jane Whitney-Smith (10)
Wybers Wood Academy, Grimsby

A Kennings Poem About Me

A kennings poem

Ace writer
Chocolate eater
Dog lover
Pom-pom maker
Good learner
Toy lover
Slow runner
Pen writer
Candy eater
Swimming learner
Steak lover
Snake lover
Sea animal lover
Animal lover
Ice eater
Toy player
Ice cream lover
Park player

Fun slider
Music lover
Good singer
Nice player
Pet owner
Trampoline master
Spider hater
Good biter.

Nancy Beatrice (7)
Wybers Wood Academy, Grimsby

This Is Me

I am caring and loving,
Like a cat protecting its kittens,
I am fearless and brave,
Like an eagle feeding its babies.

I am not afraid and timid,
Like a squirrel in a tree,
I am not shy and creepy,
Like a gazelle running from a lion.

I am passionate and courageous,
I love to care and help,
I am adventurous and ambitious,
I love to talk to new people.

Sophie Thompson (10)
Wybers Wood Academy, Grimsby

Fierce Forest Predator

A rustle in the shadowy hidden bushes
A breath in the darkness
A glimpse of steel-grey eyes
The sight of an eagle, hearing of a mouse
Claws of iron, fangs of titanium
The strength of an ox
With an attitude to match
Family protector, team player
Always helps a friend in need
Can bring down a moose
But has a big heart
When it comes to their pack
What am I?

Isobella Watts (10)
Wybers Wood Academy, Grimsby

About Me

This poem is about me
Who has never been stung by a bee
I am never usually sad
But I have a brother who is sometimes bad
My favourite colour is pink
I like to write in ink
I used to have two dogs
They always were playing with hogs
I hate logs
That are in bogs
I wish I had a cat
Who would always play with mats
I have a toy cat
And an imaginary bat.

Violet Stretton (8)
Wybers Wood Academy, Grimsby

This Is Me

I am sensible and smart,
Like Albert Einstein,
I am quick and fun,
Like birds cheeping in the woods.

I am not loud and naughty,
Like a lion roaring at its prey,
I'm not mean and horrible,
Like a piranha fish, trying to bite you.

I am helpful and courageous,
I really like to help,
I am adventurous and joyful,
I love to find out new things.

Lucas Turner (9)
Wybers Wood Academy, Grimsby

This Is Me

I am a fan of ham,
A gamer girl,
I like twirls,
I am a fan of Haribos,
I have a bow and arrow,
I am a Manchester United supporter,
I want to be a footballer,
I am only five foot size,
But I love Weetabix,
I love reading black powder,
I always make cakes from powder,
I love my game brother,
I also love my mother,
I also love my family.

Chloe Waite (10)
Wybers Wood Academy, Grimsby

This Is Me

M aking games is wonderful,
A nd creative too,
K ind of hard and tricky,
I know, I struggle too,
N ever ever give up,
G ames are always great.

G ames history could be yours,
A platform to create,
M aking games is great,
E ither one, you could pick,
S o making games is great.

Jamie (9)
Wybers Wood Academy, Grimsby

This Is Me

H ave annoying habits I am told
A nd I like football
R eally annoying
R eally lazy
Y ouTuber

F unny
L oves Clash Of Clans
E ater of chocolate
T errible at handwriting
C andle smeller
H andy when I want to be
E ar wiggler
R eally good at trampolining.

Harry Fletcher (10)
Wybers Wood Academy, Grimsby

All About Me

My name is Matilda,
This is all about me, call me Tilda,
I play sports all the time,
I am a pet lover, I have a dog called Joey, he whines when I leave,
Reading I love, it's calming and relaxing,
I like to bake and cook, it's one of my favourites,
I play football for two teams, it gets crowded easily,
That's the things you should know about me!

Matilda Reveler (10)
Wybers Wood Academy, Grimsby

Who Am I?

Very bright, with curls at the front
With goldish brown hair
I can't be beat
I'm an excellent drawer
With two feet
It's not that hard when you are me
I listen to people when they are sad
Of course they come to me because I do no bad
I may do mischief there or then
But I can assure you I'm the funniest girl you will ever meet.

Bluebell Blow (10)
Wybers Wood Academy, Grimsby

This Is Me

I am as bold as a tiger,
Like a protecting shark,
I am as quick as a blink of an eye,
Like a dragon getting its food,

I am not scared,
Like a mouse in a hole,
I am not afraid of the dark,
Like an upset rabbit,

I am as protecting as a lion,
I love being respectful,
I am caring,
I love to do different things.

Alana Bouch
Wybers Wood Academy, Grimsby

All About Isla

I'm called Isla
Bit of a crazy one
I have many friends
And love cold weather
I'm a bit clumsy
I'm a big wimp
I love school
And PE
Also computing
My favourite animal is a shark
I don't like my sister
I love family
Don't worry my friend
I love chips
Although I hate them without salt.

Isla Stainton (8)
Wybers Wood Academy, Grimsby

This Is Me

F antastic mathematician
O llie is intelligent
O liver is good at football
T ruly wonderful me
B asketball is a good sport
A sking lots of questions
L ove my life
L ots of work

K yan is amazing
Y ou are amazing
A sk for help
N ot naughty.

Kyan (9)
Wybers Wood Academy, Grimsby

This Is Me

L aughing Lilly
I ndependent, really cool
L azy, lovely and loud
L ively me, I am a busy bee
Y elling loud Lilly

D ancing and prancing
A wesome and nice
V ery bad at football
I ntelligent and hardworking
E njoyable person
S uper kind and caring.

Lilly Davies (9)
Wybers Wood Academy, Grimsby

All About Me

My name is Harley
I am very gnarly
I like football
Also basketball because I can slam dunk
I am cool, not a fool
If you think I am you are cruel
I have a dog that also sits on a log, in the fog
I have a cat that sits on my lap
I went on holiday last year
If you didn't think I did you better run away
Like a stray.

Harley Rendall-Williams
Wybers Wood Academy, Grimsby

Me

E verything Sucks is my favourite TV show
L abradorite is my favourite crystal
L unar witches are the best
A nime is very entertaining

S amsung is my type of phone
M inecraft is the best
I nternet is what I go on most
T ikTok
H aikyu is my favourite anime.

Ella Smith (10)
Wybers Wood Academy, Grimsby

This Is Me

I am burning and hot
Like a molten fire
I am fast and small
Like a cat sprinting away
I am not slow and dumb
Like a snail trying to slide away
I am not crazy and mad like thunder raging
I am clever and talented
I love to do my subject
I am adventurous and brave
I love to see the world
Like a rainbow.

Grace Li
Wybers Wood Academy, Grimsby

This Is Me

I'm Brandon,
I am very random,
I like football,
But not like going to a mall,
I'm as quick as a cheetah,
And my dream name is Peter,
I do not like sleeping,
But I like pooping,
I have a loud voice,
And my dream car is a Rolls Royce,
I like jelly,
And I like going in the mud wearing wellies.

Brandon Bore (10)
Wybers Wood Academy, Grimsby

This Is Me

There once was a boy called Adam
He went to France
Did a little dance
Came home with all the women

My favourite sport is soccer
He has a messy locker
He has a lot of mates
There is nothing he really hates
He is really kind
He hates to play up behind
He doesn't remember the last time he dived.

Adam Porter (10)
Wybers Wood Academy, Grimsby

My Life

My brother Arlo plays basketball six times a day,
But me over here sleeps in until quarter past eight,
I love to dance all day but upstairs my other brother Rueben plays GTA5 all day,
I love to play, I love to write,
But my mum or dad will rather stay up all night,
I love my birthday but I would go rollerblading with my family.

Lila-Blue Smithson (9)
Wybers Wood Academy, Grimsby

This Is Me

I am caring and confident,
Like a fox caring for her cubs,
I am bright,
Like a lamp post shining in the night.

I am not disrespectful and untrustworthy,
Like a criminal,
I am not unkind,
Like a bully,
I am cautious and aware,
Like an eagle,
I stand my ground,
Like a tree in a storm.

Leya Whitley (10)
Wybers Wood Academy, Grimsby

My Life At Dance

My friends like to prance
I dance my heart out until it's gone
Once it's gone I feel like I'm done
But I come back the next day
There's one outside I love to stare at
I bring my drink that I sometimes slurp
Then I dance and feel energy and prance
That's why I love to dance with my friends

Charlotte Waddingham-Koskie (8)
Wybers Wood Academy, Grimsby

Magical Me

I am a
Fan of ham
I love space
It is ace
I love books
I have great looks
I play sport
I think big thoughts
My favourite thing is Harry Potter
I like writing in my jotter
I am very sweet
All week, every week
I have lots of time
I hope you listen to my rhyme
This is me.

Layla Rendall (11)
Wybers Wood Academy, Grimsby

Definitely Me

Sizzling burgers,
Big, juicy and fat,
Sweet, milk, dark chocolate,
Breaking a KitKat,
Big massive hotdogs, a sausage between buns,
Cooking in the kitchen, you're annoying all the mums,
Make some fresh, cold ice cream,
Fruit without the plums,
Sweet, sugary sweets,
Sherbert and lemon!

Isabelle McKerracher (11)
Wybers Wood Academy, Grimsby

This Is Me

I am
Fun and bright
I love to drink Sprite
I'm fun
I'm like a hot dog in a bun
I'm proud
I'm loud
I stick out in a crowd
I'm smart
I like a lemon tart
I like bird nests
But I can't stand tests
I'm sporty
And I love to watch Rick and Morty.

Henry Major (11)
Wybers Wood Academy, Grimsby

This Is Me

Love to play football
I am very tall
I am super fast
I can run into the vast
I can leap so high
You wouldn't hear me say bye
I play for a team
It was a dream
You should see my big feet
I can't stay still on a seat
Also I have anger issues
But I don't use tissues.

Arthur H (10)
Wybers Wood Academy, Grimsby

This Is Me

I am strong and daring,
Like a bear in the woods,
I am athletic and sporty,
Like a leopard running through the long grass
after its prey.

I am not shy more scared to speak,
I love to make people laugh,
I am fidgety and adventurous,
I love to find new places and things to see and do.

Freddie Fawcett
Wybers Wood Academy, Grimsby

This Is Me

I am courageous and sweet,
Like sugar in a jar,
I am fast and fun,
Like a lion playing.

I am not rude and scary,
Like a poisoned snake,
I am not silent and sleepy,
Like a kitty.

I am loud and friendly,
Like a hummingbird,
I am nice and kind,
Like a puppy.

Gracie Callanan (9)
Wybers Wood Academy, Grimsby

Who Am I?

I shall be big
But my heart is small
I am cold-blooded
So don't mess with me
I can kill
I am the top predator of the chain
I live and like to give pain
I live under the sea
But now I'm ending
I am in a popular film
Who am I?

Answer: Mosasaurus.

Oliver Dee (10)
Wybers Wood Academy, Grimsby

Myself

My name is Luke, I play football
My favourite TV show is So Cobra Kia
My favourite film is Suicide Squad
I am a family person
I can easily cry
I am not that good at writing and history
I am a sporty person
I am a fast runner
I have four sisters, one brother and a dog.

Luke Taylor (11)
Wybers Wood Academy, Grimsby

This Is Me

I am musical and magical
Like a cat in a rave
I am full of passion and soul
Like a musical note
I am not shy and worried
Like a stray animal
I am never silent and voiceless
Like a parrot in a hole
I am loyal and protective
Like the queen's royal guards.

Jeremiah Blackmore (9)
Wybers Wood Academy, Grimsby

This Is Me

I play football and I'm very tall,
I eat pasta and I can run faster,
I eat chocolate it's the best for me,
I have a cat its name is Lola,
I always drink cola,
I am sporty,
And I watch Rick and Morty,
I play video games,
And sometimes it involves flames.

Leyton Jackson (10)
Wybers Wood Academy, Grimsby

Me

To make me you will need
A kitchen
To take me to football
A garden
Food
100ml of kindness in a jug

Mix a big kitchen into the mix
Take me to a football pitch
Slowly mix a garden in
Add a lot of food
Add a jug of kindness
This is me!

Ella Cooper (10)
Wybers Wood Academy, Grimsby

All About Me
A kennings poem

Roblox player
Animal lover
Sport trainer
Fastest eater
Slime player
Fortnite player
Animal Crossing player
Among Us player
Netflix watcher
YouTube watcher
Nintendo player
Dog lover
TV watcher
Teddy hugger
Minecraft player.

Poppy Oxton (7)
Wybers Wood Academy, Grimsby

Football

F eet to skill other players
O ur team uses teamwork
O ur team uses our brains
T ogether we play football
B all to play the game
A thlete that everyone knows
L eads to winning
L ands on the football pitch.

Blake Pritchard (9)
Wybers Wood Academy, Grimsby

Rap Is Me

Athletic, kind
Reliable mind
I am very happy
I am not a nappy

I like to game
I have a lot of fame
I am very bright
I am very light
I love Sprite
I like to go high
So I can touch the sky
I will never die
This is my life.

Rhys Lancaster (10)
Wybers Wood Academy, Grimsby

Me

I'm quick
I'm fast
I'm really good at maths
Whoever you are
You're special and loved
I'm special
I'm bright
I'm really really kind
I'm an animal lover
That's really really good.

This is me!

Kaila Dodd (10)
Wybers Wood Academy, Grimsby

This Is Me

What you need to make me
Boxing ring
Phone
TikTok
Bike
TV
Football

So put one boxing ring and a phone together and stir
Then add TikTok, the bike, the TV and the football
Then gently stir
That is what you need to make me.

Jack Avison (11)
Wybers Wood Academy, Grimsby

My Life

You know my nan
Sunday dinner is more like a winner
But I still eat it because I get dessert
Oh no it's broccoli
After that, I go on my mum's phone
No, homework!
I got home after my homework
I go on my Xbox
Wait, no!
Bedtime!

Alfie Sowerby (9)
Wybers Wood Academy, Grimsby

This Is Me

I am a
Lightning-quick footballer
Fabulous FIFA 22 player
I support Man City
My favourite footballer is Sergio Agüero
My dog is called Dotty
I have lots of friends
The team I hate is Manchester United
I especially hate Wayne Rooney.

Flynn Westfield (10)
Wybers Wood Academy, Grimsby

This Is Me

I am strong and powerful,
Like a crocodile eating its prey,
I am fun and musical,
Like Michael Jackson,

I am not small and shy,
Like a shadow in the sunlight,
I am not mean or horrible,
Like a poisonous snake.

This is me.

Kobi Sellar
Wybers Wood Academy, Grimsby

All About Me
A kennings poem

Animal lover
Chocolate eater
Pet owner
Long hair
Wind power
Great smiler
Teddy hugger
Benny lover
Baby carer
TV watcher
Spider hater
Game player
Cat lover
Trampoline jumper
Family lover
Vet dreamer.

Lucy Hutchinson (8)
Wybers Wood Academy, Grimsby

Stick Up For Your Rights

No matter who you are
No matter where you go
You are you
No one can change that
I stand up for my rights
When people try to bring me down
I don't stop building up
Because no one's gonna break my tower down
Because this is me!

Lucas Ardito (10)
Wybers Wood Academy, Grimsby

This Is Me

T ikToker
H elpful
I love kickboxing
S illy town is where I belong

I love bats
S mart

M erida and Celestia are the names of my guinea pigs
E mmie is my sister's name.

Elsie Jackson (11)
Wybers Wood Academy, Grimsby

Birthday

B anging, brilliant birthday
I ntelligent Riley rules
R uthless Riley laughs
T remendous birthday today
H appy great day
D ifficult different game
A mazing ancient toys
Y ellow, new top.

Riley D (10)
Wybers Wood Academy, Grimsby

Ronny's Weird Life

My name is Ronny
My dad is called Jonny
I have a cat called Bear
He likes to touch my hair
He steals people's chairs
He likes to jump in the air
Also, I like Manchester United
I know we are a bit bare
But we are up there.

Ronny Roberts (10)
Wybers Wood Academy, Grimsby

The Recipe For Me

First, add 20g of drawing,
Next stir while adding sleep time,
After add 60g of Netflix,
Let it set for thirty minutes,
Ten you have my personality,
Then add 100g of talking,
After that add 90g of cats and friends,
This is me.

Izabelle Norman (10)
Wybers Wood Academy, Grimsby

All About Emily
A kennings poem

Swimming paddler
Pub eater
Hot tub lover
Make-up lover
Good writer
Horse rider
Roblox player
Ballet dancer
Animal lover
Trampoline jumper
Painting artist
Cake eater
Slime lover
Gymnastics lover.

Emily Mai (8)
Wybers Wood Academy, Grimsby

About Me
A kennings poem

Pen writer
Amazing eater
Steak lover
Good learner
Swimming paddler
Slow runner
Fact learner
Ice cream eater
Dancing master
Reading lover
Dog and cat carer
Animal helper
Toy lover
Spider hater.

Lilly Waller (7)
Wybers Wood Academy, Grimsby

About Me
A kennings poem

Gym fighter
Energy burner
Marshall arts trainer
Karate master
Football player
Dog hater
Cat hater
Spider hater
Fast runner
Music lover
Toy player
Toy lover
Trampoline jumper
Football kicker.

Olly Holgate (8)
Wybers Wood Academy, Grimsby

About Me
A kennings poem

Chips lover
Phone player
Swimming master
Nugget lover
Trampoline liker
Cat lover
Dog liker
Xbox player
Spider hater
Popit liker
TV watcher
Pizza
Friends maker
Baby carer
Gamer pro.

Erika Ioana (7)
Wybers Wood Academy, Grimsby

About Me
A kennings poem

Book reader
Ballet dancer
Potter lover
Roblox player
Dog lover
Friend liker
Golf hater
Film watcher
Good swimmer
Doughnut eater
Beach goer
Cartwheel doer
Good splitter
School learner.

Izabelle Blanchard (7)
Wybers Wood Academy, Grimsby

This Is Me

I have a teacher called Mr Wakefield
A brother called Bobby
A sister called Lotti
A cousin called Kealan
I go to Wybers Wood Academy
I'm in Powles class
I'm always happy
I love unicorns
I'm Amber.

Amber Whitney-Smith (9)
Wybers Wood Academy, Grimsby

Calmness

If you need calmness, come to me
I will be near the little tree
The calmness with all the flowers
No need to be one of those blowers
Don't scare the bees or they will sting
Be one with the calmness of some other thing.

Lily Dodds (8)
Wybers Wood Academy, Grimsby

All About Me

I am quick,
I am fast,
I am really good at maths,
I can slam,
I can dunk,
From my hands to the net,
I love rabbits,
They have habits,
I am cool,
Not a fool,
If you think I am,
You are cruel.

Harry Smith (10)
Wybers Wood Academy, Grimsby

This Is Me

T his is me
H ave been told I'm chatty
I love my family
S our yet sweet

I ncludes everyone
S mart and kind

M arvellous
E nthusiastic and emo.

Daisy Dodds (10)
Wybers Wood Academy, Grimsby

Guess My Friend

Yes I'm a girl, does that mean I can't run
You think 'cause I'm female I can't find football fun
You assume I like pink, shopping and make-up
But get that out of your head, it's time for you to wake up!

Honey-May Bradley (10)
Wybers Wood Academy, Grimsby

Cat Poem

This is a story of a cat
Who was very fat
He always chased rats
Because he was always on mats
He never got stuff which was good
Because it was always made of wood
He was very bad
Because he always got mad.

Charlotte Porter (8)
Wybers Wood Academy, Grimsby

My School

M agnificent me
Y ou learn so much more

S hining stars
C ool kids
H ome of healthiness and happiness
O MG
O h so cool
L oving, kind, caring school.

Elizabeth Atter (9)
Wybers Wood Academy, Grimsby

About Me
A kennings poem

Movie lover
Cake eater
Swimming paddler
Drawing lover
Book reader
Gymnastics lover
Animal feeder
Good learner
Caring lover
Great smeller
Teddy lover
Hair lover
Chocolate lover.

Olivia Swales (7)
Wybers Wood Academy, Grimsby

Silly Skinned Thing

A silver-scaled thing
In the water
Moving swiftly
Jumping slowly
Propelling itself
Into flight
It sets off
With the
Wind behind
It sets itself
Back in the water
To redo the process.

Heston Bloomfield (10)
Wybers Wood Academy, Grimsby

This Is Me

M y favourite sport is football
A professional footballer
I love dancing, especially tap
S o come with me to KFC
I spend some time with my family
E xtra gravy you will see.

Maisie Sowerby (10)
Wybers Wood Academy, Grimsby

This Is Me

A dog lover, my favourite is Betsy
Someone that plays out whenever I can
A coding master
A thankful person
A football lover
A cooking expert
A scooter person
A seaside lover
A running expert.

Jack Hillman (11)
Wybers Wood Academy, Grimsby

This Is Me

I am Sophia and I am here,
I can cook while reading a book,
I have a dog and I can't vlog,
I eat pasta to get faster,
I can draw and my cat has big paws,
My favourite colour is red and I like beds.

Sophia Waddingham-Koskie (11)
Wybers Wood Academy, Grimsby

This Is My Poem

I am a superstar striker
Fabulous FIFA 22 player
I love Ronaldo
Manchester United are the best
They're better than the rest
I am a sporting footballer
I am caring, helping and a lot smaller.

Freddie Croudson (10)
Wybers Wood Academy, Grimsby

About Me
A kennings poem

Book lover
Pizza eater
Dance stepper
Horse admirer
Animal lover
Good friend
Nintendo player
Colour lover
Helpful learner
Swimming paddler
Noisy talker
Spider hater.

Erin Dalton (7)
Wybers Wood Academy, Grimsby

This Is Me

T ikTok
H elpful
I nterior designer
S ocial

I love football
S trange

M cDonald's
E lephants are my favourite animal.

Aaliyah Porritt (10)
Wybers Wood Academy, Grimsby

This Is Me

I am a
Chatty, sporty
Team player
I like to eat chocolate for tea
The seaside is alright for me
I like to spend time by the sea
Never stop running
Hesitant strong, brave, protective.

Charlie Brindley (10)
Wybers Wood Academy, Grimsby

This Is Me

I am
Caring
Kind
Like helping others
An owner of a gecko
Sporty
Hard-working
Creative
Basketball and football lover
Art lover
Talking a lot
Always have a smile.

Marley Hallam (10)
Wybers Wood Academy, Grimsby

About Me
A kennings poem

Florence Mae Gallagher
Cat lover
Tree climber
Trampoline jumper
Dog hater
Friends maker
Sister lover
Spider hater
Book reader
Toy player
TV lover
Baby hugger.

Florence Gallagher (7)
Wybers Wood Academy, Grimsby

This Is Me

R eally love reading
E xtraordinary imagination
A mazing and exciting
D aring and cruel
I ngenious
N ever-ending fun
G reat and mind-blowing.

Harrison Drinkell (9)
Wybers Wood Academy, Grimsby

About Me

I like KitKats
I like cats
I am very picky with my books
I like McDonald's chicken nuggets
I like fries, especially McDonald's ones
If you see me you'll see a phone in my hand.

Sophie Brown (10)
Wybers Wood Academy, Grimsby

What I Like!
A kennings poem

Potter lover
Film watcher
Cream eater
School learner
Book reader
Dog lover
Good swimmer
Friend liker
Beach goer
Pen writer
Minecraft gamer
Fortnite lover.

Nahla Ingram (7)
Wybers Wood Academy, Grimsby

What Do I Like?
A kennings poem

Messy crafter
Good singer
Halloween lover
Curious learner
Food liker
Ice cream taker
School hater
Book wormer
Friendly player
Awesome baker
Delightful smiler.

Freya Dee (7)
Wybers Wood Academy, Grimsby

How To Make Me

You need purple pineapple pie,
You need a pet corgi and Siberian husky,
You need lemonade,
Good handwriting,
Dark berry Tango,
Harry Potter,
Chocolate,
Now you have me!

Seren Saunders (8)
Wybers Wood Academy, Grimsby

This Is Me

L over of animals and cheese
E xciting, excellent games are all for me
O verly excited when it comes to games
N ever-ending love for games
A game lover.

Leona Cutting (9)
Wybers Wood Academy, Grimsby

What Do I Like?
A kennings poem

Music lover
Messy crafter
School liker
Bed liker
Football player
Animal lover
Silly billy
Internet liker
Halloween lover
Great crafter
Smart learner.

Dolly Barker Johnstone (8)
Wybers Wood Academy, Grimsby

This Is Me

M agnificent dancer,
A lways dancing around,
I ndependent worker,
C aring, creative person,
E xcited all of the time,
Y es, that's me.

Maicey Bateman (10)
Wybers Wood Academy, Grimsby

Who Is It?
A kennings poem

Cardboard eater
Sibling fighter
Wallpaper tearer
Carpet ripper
Hay lover
Tunnel user
Small hopper
Fast runner
What am I?

Answer: My bunny Ronnie.

Ellie Clough (8)
Wybers Wood Academy, Grimsby

Who Am I?
A kennings poem

Pizza lover
Messy bessy
Lazy Daisy
Silly billy
Curious person
Friendly friend
Good eater
Ice cream licker
Pet lover
Halloween lover
Christmas lover.

Olivia Westerman (8)
Wybers Wood Academy, Grimsby

Who Am I?
A kennings poem

Awesome person
Intelligent learner
Great gamer
Polite person
Messy crafter
Silly person
Ice cream lover
Football lover
Basketball lover
Chocolate lover.

Levi Whitton (8)
Wybers Wood Academy, Grimsby

Skeletons

I am a skeleton
I used to have skin
I rose from the grave
Not from the bin
I really like chocolate
Too bad I can't eat
I am a skeleton
Why don't we meet?

Riley Waters (9)
Wybers Wood Academy, Grimsby

This Is Me

I like maps
This is a rap
Awesome
Kind
I like to rhyme
I like food
I am not rude
I have a puppy
His name is Woody
I like burgers
With no salad.

Dexter Todd
Wybers Wood Academy, Grimsby

About Me
A kennings poem

Potter lover
Sushi eater
Ball kicker
Football player
Singer liker
Karate liker
Goalkeeper
Sport lover
Nintendo player
Writer liker
Maths liker.

Oscar Thompson (7)
Wybers Wood Academy, Grimsby

All About Me

T remendous Tom so full of life
H appy all day and night
O f course I play Fortnite
M arvellous at games
A lways playing
S uperstar.

Thomas Mills (10)
Wybers Wood Academy, Grimsby

Who Am I?
A kennings poem

Smart learner
Friendly person
Fearless person
Curious person
Fun learner
Messy person
Chocolate lover
Silly person
Football lover
Curious learner.

Harley Oakshatt (7)
Wybers Wood Academy, Grimsby

What Do I Love?
A kennings poem

Water lover
Football lover
Basketball lover
Running lover
Ruby lover
Game watcher
Football watcher
Athletics lover
Fruit lover
Watermelon lover.

Jacob Taylor (8)
Wybers Wood Academy, Grimsby

About Me
A kennings poem

Minecraft gamer
Pokémon trader
JLT lover
McDonald's eater
Karate fighter
Trampoline flipper
Ace defender
Maths learner
Basketball player.

Oscar Capindale (7)
Wybers Wood Academy, Grimsby

All About Me
A kennings poem

Blonde hairer
Slower writer
Annoying brother
TikTok liker
Fortnite player
Demon child
Potter lover
Minecraft hacker
Craft master
Food lover.

Isla Penny Anderson-Bright (7)
Wybers Wood Academy, Grimsby

All About Elianna
A kennings poem

Candy lover
Book reader
Game hoster
Pen writer
Nature flower
Beautiful dancer
Roblox player
Animal jammer
Fantasy dreamer
Buttercup picker.

Elianna Greetham (7)
Wybers Wood Academy, Grimsby

About Me
A kennings poem

Minecraft player
Good swimmer
Football scorer
Food eater
McDonald's eater
Spider killer
Pen writer
Writing lover
Dog lover
TV lover.

George Mazingham (7)
Wybers Wood Academy, Grimsby

Who Am I?
A kennings poem

Silly billy
Football player
Book lover
Messy crafter
Cool gamer
Awesome friend
Lovely person
Fun worker
Brave adventurer
Funny person.

Daisy Grimble-Wright (7)
Wybers Wood Academy, Grimsby

Guess What It Is

Flesh ripper
Voltage breather
Shiny scales
Awesome speed
Bolted energy
Terrific claws
Ultimate killer
Spiky leaver

Electric dragon.

Kealan Croft (8)
Wybers Wood Academy, Grimsby

This Is Me

A mazing at football
R eally fast runner
C lever at maths
H aving fun in football
I love science
E njoying football.

Archie (9)
Wybers Wood Academy, Grimsby

What Am I Like?
A kennings poem

Awesome friend
Messy boy
Smart human
Curious thinker
Fun person
Fearless soul
Helpful body
Ice cream adorer
Great biker
Book reader.

William Lewis (7)
Wybers Wood Academy, Grimsby

Who Am I?
A kennings poem

Puppy lover
Llama liker
Penguin liker
Book worm
Silly billy
Curious thinker
Excellent painter
Nice partner
Crazy dancer
Fun player.

Ava Kirwan (8)
Wybers Wood Academy, Grimsby

Who Am I?
A kennings poem

Silly billy
Great gamer
Lego builder
TV watcher
Awesome friend
Crazy crafter
Pig lover
Sleeping lover
Creative person
Candy eater.

Walter Holdsworth (8)
Wybers Wood Academy, Grimsby

What Am I Like?
A kennings poem

Fun loving
Music lover
Curious learner
Friendly girl
Silly billy
Daydreamer
Awesome dancer
Cool friend
Pillow fighter
Book worm.

Chloe Smith (7)
Wybers Wood Academy, Grimsby

About Me

A kennings poem

Liverpool lover
Football gamer
Noodle eater
KitKat scoffer
Doughnut liker
Ace learner
Sweet lover
Fortnite player
Nintendo liker.

Freddie Colyer (7)
Wybers Wood Academy, Grimsby

Who Am I?
A kennings poem

Curious listener
Music hearer
Good eater
Passionate person
Ocean explorer
Amazing builder
Holiday lover
Halloween girl
Dog liker.

Millie McKerracher (8)
Wybers Wood Academy, Grimsby

Who Am I?

A kennings poem

Playstation player
Sweet lover
Smart learner
Math lover
Silly billy
Basketball player
Friendly person
Fun lover
Halloween lover.

Darren Richardson (8)
Wybers Wood Academy, Grimsby

What Am I Like?
A kennings poem

Bath dreamer
Shower hater
Silly billy
Neat bedroomer
Positive learner
Sleepover power
Pet lover
Book wormer
Strawberry sweeter.

Hattie Acquorff (8)
Wybers Wood Academy, Grimsby

This Is Me

M arvellous and magnificent
A mazing and anxious
S uper like Spider-Man
O bliging and radiant
N ice and respectful.

Mason Howarth (9)
Wybers Wood Academy, Grimsby

All About Me
A kennings poem

I am a,
Football superstar,
Pet lover,
Meat eater,
Book reader,
Veg hater,
FIFA player,
Shy,
Intelligent,
Gut follower.

Lucas Freeman (10)
Wybers Wood Academy, Grimsby

Who Am I?
A kennings poem

Smart learner
Silly friend
Fearless person
Slow eater
Mushroom lover
Basketball player
Cake hater
Bookwormer
Drawing maker.

Oliver Smith (8)
Wybers Wood Academy, Grimsby

This Is Me

I am brave and fearless,
Like a bear protecting its cubs,
I am speedy and brawny,
Like a bird scouting out its prey.

This is me.

Kyle White (9)
Wybers Wood Academy, Grimsby

About Me
A kennings poem

Food lover
Baby lover
Bed lover
Morning hater
Cup of tea lover
Coffee hater
Art lover
Fresh air lover
Sun hater.

Milla Robinson (7)
Wybers Wood Academy, Grimsby

Who Am I?
A kennings poem

Angry shouter
Messy eater
Book lover
Smart learner
Passionate role model
Friendly human
Dog lover
Curious friend.

Hannah Tobis (8)
Wybers Wood Academy, Grimsby

What Am I Like?
A kennings poem

Fun friend
Messy footballer
Awesome gamer
Friendly human
Smart pupil
Curious student
Dog lover
Teddy collector.

Jack Ward (8)
Wybers Wood Academy, Grimsby

What Am I?
A kennings poem

Silly person
Angry human
Smart concentrator
Awesome gamer
Fearless brother
Messy mudder
Story lover
Cake liker.

Theo Porter (8)
Wybers Wood Academy, Grimsby

What Am I Like?
A kennings poem

Friendly human
Messy eater
Smart mammal
Fun player
Expert entertainer
Cookie lover
Dog player
Football lover.

Harry Corke (8)
Wybers Wood Academy, Grimsby

My Pet Rabbit Rosie

A kennings poem

Treat eater
Cardboard destroyer
Fast runner
Small hopper
Good stretcher
Hay lover
Tunnel user
Loving helper.

Grace Hydes (8)
Wybers Wood Academy, Grimsby

About Me
A kennings poem

Pizza lover
Minecraft player
Game player
Ice cream eater
Dog hater
Mushroom hater
Xbox player
Pen wanter.

Benji West (8)
Wybers Wood Academy, Grimsby

Who Am I?
A kennings poem

Football lover
Awesome gamer
Fearless person
Cat lover
Silly billy
Cookie lover
Kind kid
Card collector.

Hayden Wood (8)
Wybers Wood Academy, Grimsby

About Me
A kennings poem

McDonald's lover
Swimming master
Roblox player
iPhone 13 Pro gamer
KFC eater
Pepsi Max liker
TV watcher.

Ben Lawson (7)
Wybers Wood Academy, Grimsby

Who Am I?
A kennings poem

Silly billy
Loving kind
Pet lover
Nice person
Swimming lover
Fun enjoyer
Christmas lover
Family lover.

Lyla Reid (9)
Wybers Wood Academy, Grimsby

This Is Me
A kennings poem

Cracker eater
Human copier
Flappy wings
Colourful bird
Beak snapper
What was it?

Answer: A parrot.

Albert Holdsworth (8)
Wybers Wood Academy, Grimsby

Who Am I?
A kennings poem

Passionate person
Silly billy
Awesome friend
Never angry
Game lover
McDonald's eater
Christmas lover.

Olivia Harris (8)
Wybers Wood Academy, Grimsby

About Me
A kennings poem

Game lover
Book reader
Xbox player
Ace defender
Demon sister
Master swimmer
Best eater
Good boxer.

Charlie Crome (7)
Wybers Wood Academy, Grimsby

All About Me
A kennings poem

Game winner
Football lover
Doughnut liker
Ace defender
Good player
Fortnite lover
Swimming master.

Isaac George Woolsey (7)
Wybers Wood Academy, Grimsby

What Am I Like
A kennings poem

Friendly person
Book lover
Messy crafter
Silly billy
Smart learner
Mess maker
Teddy collector.

Phoebe Spendlow (7)
Wybers Wood Academy, Grimsby

Who Am I?
A kennings poem

Story lover
Awesome person
Music dancer
Silly billy
Family lover
Good friend
Birthday lover.

Rose Dodds (7)
Wybers Wood Academy, Grimsby

What About Me

A kennings poem

Messy sister
Ice cream stealer
Lonely child
Silly mum
Angry person
Art lover
Football hater.

Amelia Peacock (8)
Wybers Wood Academy, Grimsby

My Life Is Games
A kennings poem

Super gamer
Minecraft lover
Fortnite Dreamer
FIFA kicker
Xbox gamer
Switch gamer
PS5 gamer.

Reuben MacFarlane (8)
Wybers Wood Academy, Grimsby

Who Am I?
A kennings poem

Gym girl
Friendly person
Book worm
Excellent reader
Silly billy
Messy pup
Food hoover.

Evie Parker (8)
Wybers Wood Academy, Grimsby

Dragon
A kennings poem

Fire breather
Tree stomper
Scary biter
Tail whipper
Wing flapper
Strong snapper.

Beau Shore (9)
Wybers Wood Academy, Grimsby

Who Am I?

A kennings poem

Silly billy
School lover
Music lover
Halloween lover
Chocolate lover
Dog lover.

Honey-Rae Phillips (8)
Wybers Wood Academy, Grimsby

Who Am I?

A kennings poem

Awesome person
Friendly boy
Smart learner
Messy crafter
Silly billy
Nice boy.

Thomas Ayres (8)
Wybers Wood Academy, Grimsby

Who Loves October

O ctober loving
L ively chaser
L onely sleeper
Y es choosing.

Olly Ranyard (8)
Wybers Wood Academy, Grimsby

About Me

A kennings poem

Princess lover
Silly chatterer
Sweet eater
Bubblegum lover.

This is me!

Esmai Rendall (7)
Wybers Wood Academy, Grimsby

What I Like
A kennings poem

Awesome human
Cooking liker
Terrific handwriter
Super helper
Guacamole lover.

Jacob Burton (8)
Wybers Wood Academy, Grimsby

Who Am I?
A kennings poem

Ice cream lover
Fun lover
Messy crafter
Silly billy
Funny bunny.

Jayden Lister (8)
Wybers Wood Academy, Grimsby

About Me
A kennings poem

Pet lover
Rabbit lover
Pet owner
Tarantula hater
Unicorn lover.

Isabella Grainger (7)
Wybers Wood Academy, Grimsby

Who Am I?

A kennings poem

School lover
Xbox player
Silly eater
Kong liker
Godzilla hater.

Frankie Leahy (8)
Wybers Wood Academy, Grimsby

YoungWriters
Est. 1991

YOUNG WRITERS INFORMATION

We hope you have enjoyed reading this book – and that you will continue to in the coming years.

If you're the parent or family member of an enthusiastic poet or story writer, do visit our website www.youngwriters.co.uk/subscribe and sign up to receive news, competitions, writing challenges and tips, activities and much, much more! There's lots to keep budding writers motivated!

If you would like to order further copies of this book, or any of our other titles, then please give us a call or order via your online account.

Young Writers
Remus House
Coltsfoot Drive
Peterborough
PE2 9BF
(01733) 890066
info@youngwriters.co.uk

Join in the conversation!
Tips, news, giveaways and much more!

YoungWritersUK   YoungWritersCW   youngwriterscw